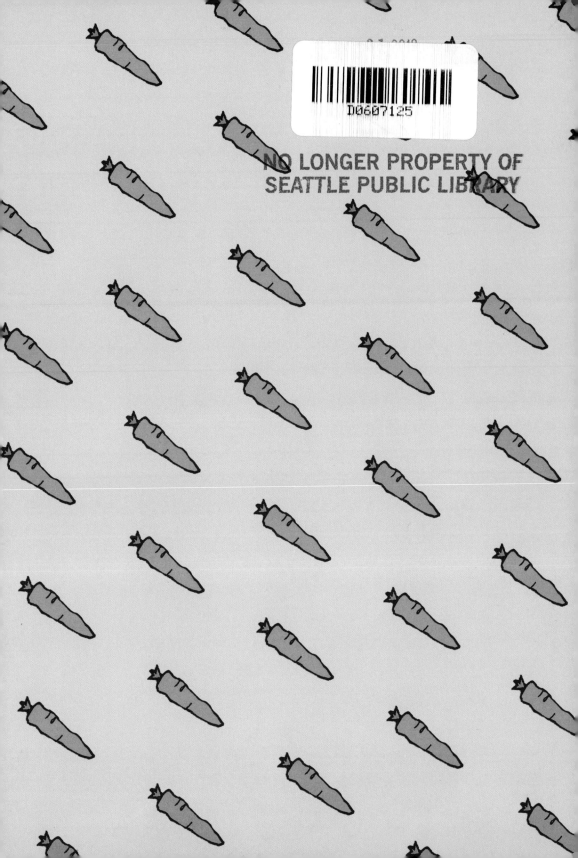

What This Story Needs Is a Munch and a Crunch

Library of Congress Control Number: 2015947624
ISBN 978-0-06-241529-5

The artist used charcoal sketches painted digitally to create the illustrations for this book.
Typography by Dana Fritts
16 17 18 19 20 SCP 10 9 8 7 6 5 4 3 2 1
❖ First Edition

WHAT THIS STORY NEEDS IS

A MUNCH AND A CRUNCH

By Emma J. Virján

HARPER

An Imprint of HarperCollinsPublishers

What this story needs is
a pig in a wig,

baking bread,

pouring punch,

and meeting a friend
for a picnic lunch.

This story also needs
a blanket,

some plates,

a few carrots

and pies,

some sandwiches,

apples,

ketchup and fries,

a game of catch,

a kite in the breeze,

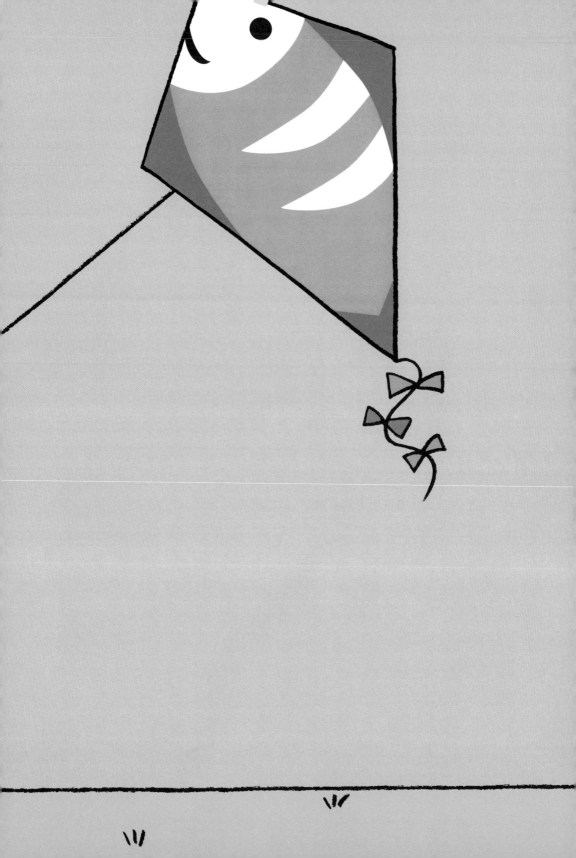

and good friends
munching and crunching
by the trees.

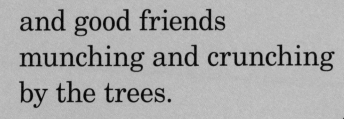

What this story needs now
is a mad dash!

Quick!
Grab the blanket,
plates, carrots,
and pies,

the sandwiches,
apples, ketchup
and fries.

What this story needs now is . . . .

another place to eat.

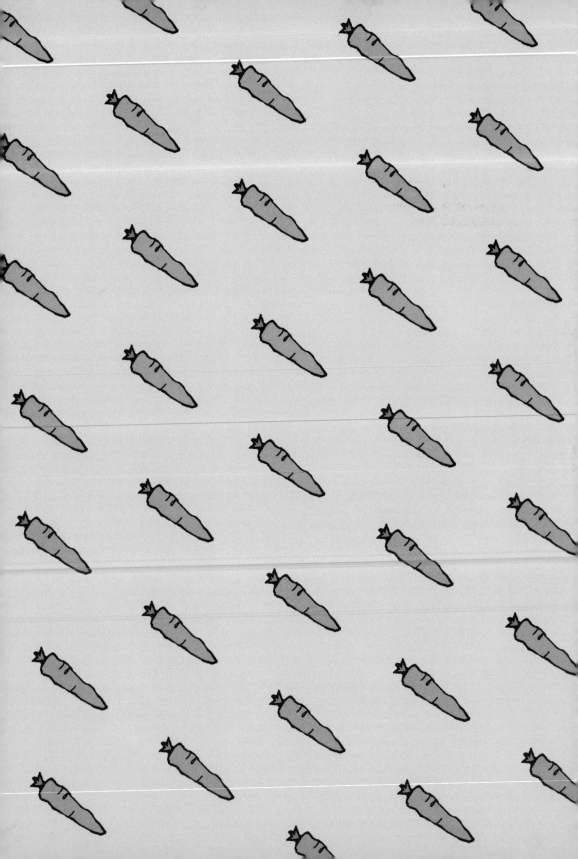